READY TO CROSS?
LOOK BOTH WAYS.
AND NO SCRIBBLING!
PUNCTUATION PATROL
PUNCTUATION PATROL
PUNCTUATION PATROL
PENCIL XING

PENCIL SCHOOL NEWS

"We get to the point"

TODAY WE CELEBRATE
WRITE ON! DAY

WHAT'S YOUR STORY?

Design by Kristine Brogno.

Typeset in Type No. 1 Regular. The illustrations in this book were rendered in watercolors, pencil and collage.

Manufactured in China.

NATIONAL PENCIL DAY is MARCH 30

Library of Congress Cataloging-in-Publication Data available.

ISBN 978-0-8118-7869-2

This book does not condone the use of explosives for any purpose other than the purely fictional.

FOR THE GROVER GIRLS:
LORIE ANN, ELLEN, EMILY
—J. H.

TO THE ALPHABET,
MY FAVORITE NOUN.
—M.S.

MIX
Paper from responsible sources
FSC
www.fsc.org   FSC® C104723

10 9 8 7 6 5 4 3 2 1
Chronicle Books LLC
680 Second Street
San Francisco, California 94107

www.chroniclekids.com

little REd writing

WRITE
OFTEN
AND
CARRY
A BIG
NOTEBOOK

chronicle books · san francisco

by
Joan Holub

pictures by
Melissa Sweet

PENCILVANIA SCHOOL

Once upon a time in pencil school, a teacher named Ms. 2 told her class, "Today we're going to write a story!"

ABCDEFGHIJ

STORY PATH
1. Idea, characters, setting
2. Trouble
3. Even bigger trouble
4. Fix the trouble

YiPPEE!

said the birthday pencil.

SLAMMiN'.

said the basketball pencil.

SHARP!

said Little Red.

said the birthday pencil.

said the state pencil.

said the basketball pencil.

wondered Little Red.

Ms. 2 gave Little Red a basket of 15 red words to use in case she ran into trouble.

said Little Red.

Once there was a **brave** red pencil who went on a journey. As she walked along....

WALKING IS BORING.

decided Little Red.

She wanted her story to be exciting!

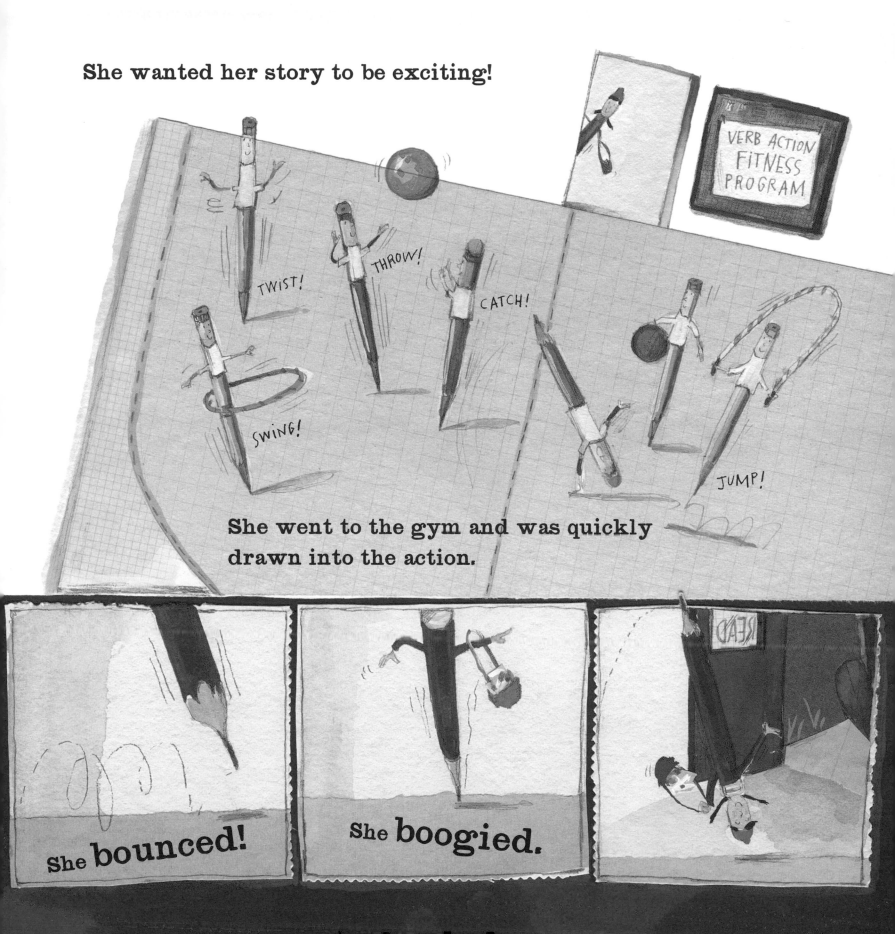

She went to the gym and was quickly
drawn into the action.

She bounced!

She boogied.

Then she cartwheeled right off the page and into...

a deep,
dark,
descriptive
forest.

DARK

PEN...

DEEP

BOSK...

SQUIRRELLY

Russet

mossy

"Description adds pizzazz to any story, but Little Red was **bogged down, hindered, lost!** She reached into her word basket for help.

AHA! SCISSORS! I NEED TO CUT THROUGH ALL THIS DESCRIPTION AND STICK TO THE STORY PATH.

scissors

LEAFY

LEA...

said a voice from
the supply closet.

Little Red squeezed the bottle . . .

Too many glue words came out!
So that is how she found herself
writing a sentence that would not
end but just kept going and going
and running on and on although
it had no purpose yet it would not
get out of her story or say anything
important so she was glad when a
helpful word arrived—

SUDDENLY
(and it brought some friends).

ADVERBS
WE DELIVER SPEEDILY

SUDDENLY, ABRUPTLY & Surprisingly,

she heard a strange sound, which she decided required all capitals and rather large punctuation:

GGRRG!!! RR-RRR

It was the middle of her story, where something exciting should happen. And it did.

That growly sound chased her!

abandoning all rules of punctuation and sentence structure in her panic to escape Little Red began running on and on and on she grabbed random nouns from her word basket tossing them out to fill up the chasm of blank space nothingness which was all that stood between her and that GRRR then hooray finally at last the page was full and she could leave the horrid sound behind and go to

...the next page. But as the page turned, Little Red couldn't help noticing a long, tangly tail disappear around the corner.

STOP

stop

nouns

card...

rose

lipstick

Was that tail up to no good?
A truly brave pencil would
follow it to find out, she thought.

She decided to tail that tail and wound up trailing it around an entire page of her story.

ATLAN

SCHOOL
CLUBS

MON.	FONTS ARE FUN
TUES.	COOKING: PENCILICIOUS RECIPES
WED.	CROSSWORD CAPERS
THUR.	SEWING: PENCIL SKIRTS

13   14 3°   15   16   17   18   19

S
T
U
V
W 39°
X
Y
Z

CAFETERIA

MR. WOODCUTTER

MUSIC ROOM

STUDENTS CELEBRATE
PENCIL POLLOCK

MR. DOODLES

ART ROOM

ROOM MATH
1|2|3

PENCIL THEATER PRESENTS
PETER PENCIL

Eventually it led her all the way to the next page and went into...

the principal's office!

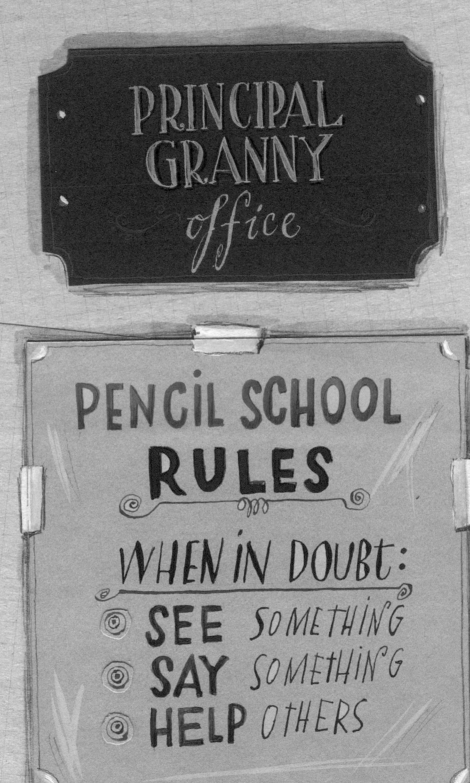

Little Red knocked on the door.

"Come in," said a growly voice.

Little Red was suspicious.

the Wolf 3000™: the grumpiest, growliest, grindingest pencil sharpener ever made!

Just as the Wolf 3000 began to chase Little Red, in walked Mr. Woodcutter, the janitor.

cried Little Red.

Mr. Woodcutter fainted.

It was up to Little Red to stop the Wolf 3000's rampage. She reached into her word basket. There was only one red noun left.

Would it do the trick?

She took aim and threw!

Luckily, Principal Granny was all right.
(Though her life had been somewhat shortened
by her experience with the Wolf 3000.)

I WASN'T REALLY BRAVE. I WAS SCARED.

said Little Red.

EVEN HEROES GET SCARED, BUT THEY DO BRAVE DEEDS ANYWAY. YOU ARE A HERO IN MY BOOK!

replied Principal Granny.

Little Red zoomed back to her classroom just in time to hear the other pencils share the stories they had written.

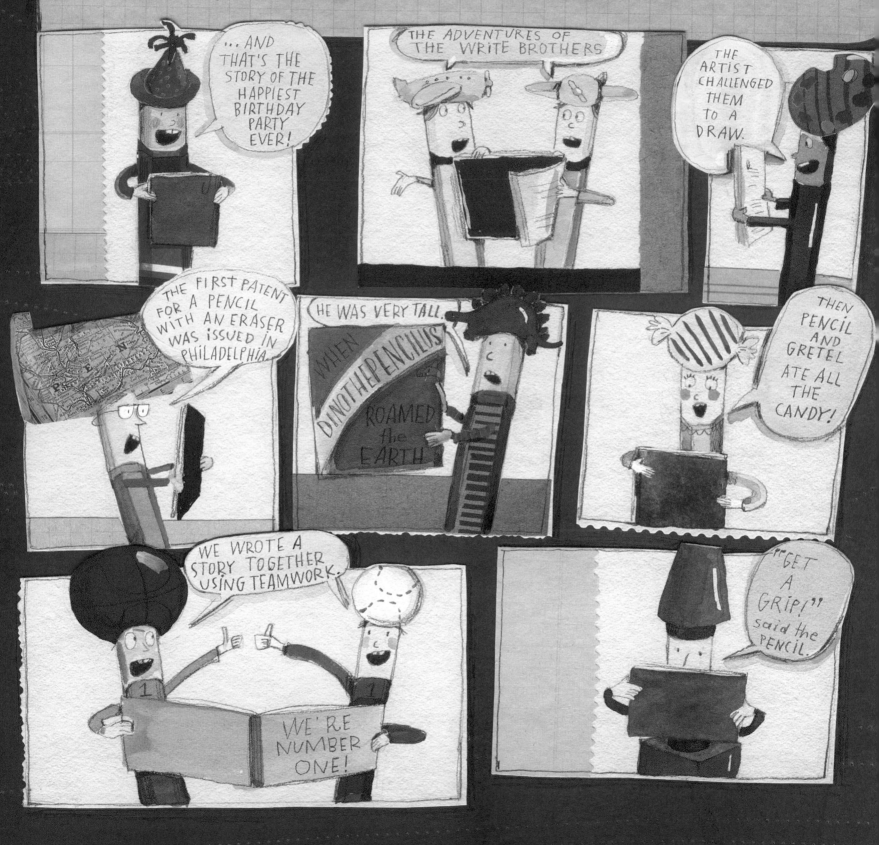

Then it was her turn.

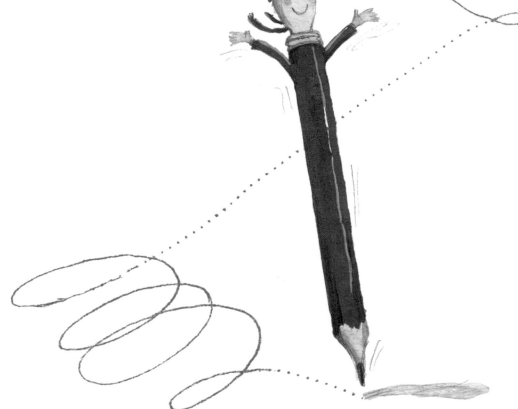